The Boxcar Children Mysteries

THE MYSTERY OF
THE SPIDER'S CLUE

created by
GERTRUDE CHANDLER WARNER

Illustrated by Hodges Soileau

SCHOLASTIC INC.
New York Toronto London Auckland Sydney
New Delhi Mexico City Hong Kong Buenos Aires

ISBN 0-439-35370-X

12 11 10 9 8 7 6 5 4 3 2   6 7/0

Printed in the U.S.A.   40
First Scholastic printing, March 2002

Contents

CHAPTER 1

Sam the Window Man

"Don't forget about the ladder," said Benny Alden. "You didn't forget it, did you, Violet?"

Violet, who was ten, smiled at her six-year-old brother. "No, I didn't, Benny," she said. She looked down at her drawing of a man on a bike. There was a ladder lashed to the top of the bike, and there were pails hanging over the handlebars. "How could I forget Sam's ladder?"

"You're doing a great job, Violet," said twelve-year-old Jessie. "That looks just like

Sam Snow, with his silver hair and his droopy mustache."

"And that's exactly the way Sam's bike looks, too," Henry pointed out. "Violet even remembered Sam's old rags tied to the ladder." At fourteen, Henry was the oldest of the Aldens.

"You really are a wonderful artist, Violet," Jessie said with pride.

Violet smiled gratefully at her older sister. "I think I *am* getting better," she said in her soft voice. "But I still have a lot to learn." Violet enjoyed drawing. And she was good at it, too.

It was a sunny afternoon, and the four Aldens — Henry, Jessie, Violet, and Benny — were sitting under a shady tree on the back lawn. They were making a special get-well card for their friend Sam the Window Man. Violet was drawing a picture to go on the front. The other Aldens were making up a poem to go inside. The Aldens' dog, Watch, was dozing in the sun nearby.

Benny took a close look at Violet's picture. "Purple?" His eyebrows suddenly shot up. "Does Sam use *purple* rags for washing windows?" he asked.

Violet laughed a little. "Probably not." Purple was Violet's favorite color, and she almost always wore something purple or violet. "But I wanted to make everything very colorful," she explained.

"That was a good idea," said Jessie. "Bright colors are very cheery."

Benny looked over at their boxcar, with its coat of bright red paint. "Our old home always makes *me* feel cheery."

Jessie brushed her hand across Benny's hair. "It always make me feel cheery, too," she said.

After their parents had died, the Aldens had found an old abandoned boxcar in the woods. The boxcar was their home for a while until their grandfather found them. That's when James Alden brought his grandchildren to live with him in his big white house in Greenfield. And the boxcar had come along, too. Now it had a special place in the backyard. The Aldens often used their old home as a clubhouse.

"I'm almost done." Violet was adding a rainbow to her picture. "It should only take me another minute or two to finish."

"I wish we could say the same thing," said Jessie, sighing. "Making up poems isn't easy. The important thing is to let Sam know that the whole town misses him."

"*And* that we want him to get better soon," added Benny.

For a moment, no one said a word. They were all too busy thinking. Jessie finally spoke up. "Maybe we could start out like this: *With ladder and bucket, you ride through the town —* "

After a pause, Benny put in, "*Washing our windows —* "

"*Upstairs and down!*" finished Henry.

Violet clapped her hands. "That sounds great!"

"Do you really think so?" Benny asked, and Violet nodded.

"I'll jot it down in my notebook," Jessie said. "Then we won't forget how it goes."

"Good thinking," said Henry. They could always count on Jessie to be organized.

Benny was grinning from ear to ear. "I told you we could do it! Making up poems is easy once you get the hang of it."

Sure enough, it didn't take the children long to finish. After Jessie copied their poem onto the get-well card, she read it out loud.

> *With ladder and bucket,*
> *You ride through the town,*
> *Washing our windows,*
> *Upstairs and down.*
> *You make everything sparkle,*
> *Wherever you go,*
> *So get well very soon,*
> *We miss you, Sam Snow!*

The children each signed their names to the card.

"I hope Sam does get better soon," said Benny.

Jessie nodded. "We all hope so, Benny. It

won't be the same without Sam the Window Man riding all over town."

"That's for sure," said Henry. "Grandfather says Sam's been washing windows in Greenfield for almost forty years."

Benny looked over at Henry. "Did Sam get hurt falling off a ladder?"

Henry shook his head. "He got hurt falling off his bike. A dog ran out into the street right in front of him," he explained. "When Sam swerved away, he ran into a tree."

Benny frowned. "Sam will get better, won't he?"

"Don't worry, Benny." Henry put his arm around his younger brother. "Sam hurt his hip when he fell. He's supposed to take it easy for a few weeks. But the doctor says he'll be fine."

"Oh, I hope so!" said Benny. Then he added, "I can't wait to give Sam our get-well card."

"We'll walk over there a bit later," Jessie told him. "Just as soon as Mrs. Mc-

Gregor's cookies are out of the oven." Mrs. McGregor was the Aldens' housekeeper and a wonderful cook.

Benny sniffed the air. "I can smell chocolate chips."

"Oh, Benny!" Violet teased. "I think you could smell food a mile away."

"*Ten* miles away," said Benny.

They all laughed. The youngest Alden was always hungry.

They laughed even harder when Benny added, "Maybe I should sample one of those cookies for Mrs. McGregor." He jumped to his feet. "Just to be sure they turned out okay."

"Mrs. McGregor's cookies always turn out okay," Henry reminded him. "In fact, they always turn out great."

But Benny wasn't listening. He was already racing full speed across the lawn, with Watch close behind.

Violet began to gather up her colored pencils. "I hope our card makes Sam smile," she said.

"I'm sure it will," Henry told her. "And if

it doesn't do the trick, Mrs. McGregor's cookies will."

"That's true," agreed Jessie. She helped Violet slip her colored pencils into a pencil case. "I hope so, anyway," she added. "Sam hasn't been very cheery lately."

"I know," said Henry. "He says he's turning into an old grouch."

Jessie laughed. She knew Sam Snow could never be an old grouch. He had a smile and a kind word for everyone. He always said he didn't have customers — he had friends. "Sam enjoys working," she said. "It must be hard for him to take it easy."

Violet nodded. "He really loves his job. He even washes windows for free sometimes. Especially for older people on tight budgets."

Henry, Jessie, and Violet were still talking about Sam when Benny came racing back across the lawn. He slid to a stop, staring wide-eyed at his brother and sisters.

"That was fast, Benny," observed Henry. "Did Mrs. McGregor's cookies pass the test?" he added with a twinkle in his eye.

Benny blinked. "Oops! I forgot all about the cookies."

The other Aldens looked at one another in surprise. It wasn't like Benny to forget about food.

Jessie looked worried. "What is it, Benny?" She often acted like a mother to her younger brother and sister.

Benny's big eyes grew even rounder. "Mrs. McGregor just told me something," he said. "Something very strange!"

"What was it?" Henry wanted to know.

Benny knelt down on the grass. "Mrs. McGregor told me Sam got an invitation in the mail today!"

Violet looked puzzled. "What's strange about that, Benny?"

Benny leaned closer. "It was an invitation to a mystery!"

Henry gave a low whistle. "I've never heard of being *invited* to a mystery."

"It *is* odd," Violet said.

"Sam's hoping we'll help him," Benny went on. "He knows we like mysteries."

Henry spoke for them all. "Of course we'll help!"

"Did Mrs. McGregor say anything else?" Jessie wanted to know.

Benny shook his head. "She was talking to Sam on the phone when I went inside. She only stopped long enough to tell me about the invitation."

Jessie wondered out loud, "Who in the world would send out an invitation to a mystery?"

"I'm sure Sam will tell us all about it when we see him today," answered Henry.

"Let's go over there right now!" Benny suggested. The youngest Alden never liked to be kept in suspense. "What are we waiting for?"

"Mrs. McGregor," Henry reminded him. "She's going with us, remember?"

"Then let's go see if Mrs. McGregor's ready to — "

Before Benny could finish the thought, Jessie was on her feet and sprinting across the lawn, Violet at her heels.

Henry raced after them, saying, "Come on, Benny!"

The children found Mrs. McGregor in the kitchen.

"Something sure smells good in here!" said Henry.

Mrs. McGregor smiled over at them. "The cookies are still warm from the oven," she said as she tied a red ribbon around a bag of cookies. "Just the way Sam likes them."

"Just the way *I* like them, too," put in Benny.

Mrs. McGregor took a quick glance at the clock. "Are you almost ready to walk over?"

Jessie laughed. "That's just what we were going to ask you."

Before they left, Benny showed Mrs. McGregor their get-well card. "We made it ourselves," he told her proudly.

Mrs. McGregor caught her breath when she saw Violet's drawing. "What a fine picture of Sam, Violet." She opened the card and read the poem. "Goodness, I had no idea the Aldens were such wonderful poets!"

"Oh, we are!" said Benny. "We're poets and we didn't even know it."

They all laughed at Benny's funny rhyme.

They said good-bye to Watch. Then Henry, Jessie, Violet, and Benny filed out the door behind Mrs. McGregor.

Sam's little yellow house was just a short walk from the Aldens'. As they got closer, the children noticed a car parked in Sam's driveway.

Violet hesitated. "It looks like Sam already has company," she said. "Maybe we should come back another time."

Benny looked disappointed. "But we're almost at Sam's house," he pointed out. "And we brought a card — and cookies!"

"That's true," said Mrs. McGregor. "We really should stop in for a moment."

Just then, something caught Jessie's eye. Across the street, a heavyset man was standing on the curb, his eyes fixed on the little yellow house. The man had silver hair —

just like Sam's. When he noticed Jessie watching him, he ducked behind the trees.

"Did you see that?" Jessie whispered to Henry.

"See what?"

"Somebody was standing over there," she told him in a low voice. "When he saw us, he disappeared."

"He was probably a friend of Sam's," guessed Henry. "Maybe he decided to come back later, when Sam doesn't have so much company."

"Maybe so," said Jessie. But she didn't sound very sure. The man had disappeared too quickly — almost as though he'd been caught doing something he shouldn't. Jessie couldn't shake the feeling that something wasn't quite right.

CHAPTER 2

The Strange Invitation

Benny rang Sam's bell. A moment later, the door opened. A man in a business suit greeted them. He was very tall, with gray hair that circled a bald spot.

"You must be Mrs. McGregor," the man said with a friendly smile. "And I bet these are the famous Alden children." He held out his hand. "I'm Thomas Paintner. An old friend of Sam's."

"I've often heard Sam speak of you," Mrs. McGregor said warmly. "And you're quite right. I'm Mrs. McGregor and these are the

15

Aldens — Henry, Jessie, Violet, and Benny."

They all shook hands. "It's nice to meet you, Mr. Paintner," the children said politely.

"None of that formal stuff," Sam's old friend told them. "Please call me Thomas."

"We'll only be staying a moment," said Mrs. McGregor. "We don't want to intrude."

Thomas shook his head as he ushered them inside. "You won't be intruding," he said. "Besides, I can only stay a little while longer myself."

The well-dressed man led them into the living room, where the afternoon sun shone through sparkling clean windows. Sam was resting on the couch, a faded old quilt thrown over him, his shirtsleeves rolled up and a cane nearby.

"I was hoping you could make it!" he said cheerfully as they came into the room.

Mrs. McGregor held up her paper bag. "I remembered your favorite cookies, Sam."

Benny's mouth dropped open as he looked around. Every square inch of every table was covered with get-well cards!

When she saw the look of surprise on Benny's face, Mrs. McGregor smiled and said, "Sam's been flooded with cards and phone calls since his accident."

"Oh, yes!" put in Sam as he propped himself up higher on the pillows. "Folks have been real good to me. Even Thomas dropped everything and came right over. I called him the minute I saw his name on that invitation."

Jessie and Henry exchanged glances. What did Thomas Paintner have to do with the strange invitation?

Mrs. McGregor said, "Why don't I make a pot of tea. Then we can sit down and have a nice visit."

Sam smoothed his droopy mustache and grinned a little. "Do you think we could have some cookies with that tea?"

Mrs. McGregor was already halfway to the kitchen. "Of course!" she called back over her shoulder.

The Aldens went along to help. While Mrs. McGregor put water on to boil, Benny arranged the cookies on a plate, Jessie poured four glasses of milk, Henry reached into the cupboard for the napkins and the teacups, and Violet filled the sugar bowl.

They made their way back to the living room. Henry helped clear a space on the coffee table for the tea tray.

Benny perched on a wooden footstool. "Will you tell us about the invitation now, Sam?" He couldn't wait to hear all about the mystery.

"Sure thing." With a nod of his head, Sam pulled an engraved invitation from his shirt pocket. He held it up for everyone to see. "This is it," he said. "I got it in the mail today."

Henry, Jessie, and Violet sat down together on the quilt-draped love seat, while Mrs. McGregor settled into one of the rocking chairs by the window. They waited expectantly for Sam to continue.

"My first thought," Sam went on, "was that it was some kind of practical joke. That's why I asked Thomas to stop by."

"It's definitely not a practical joke," Thomas said firmly. "There's a lot of money waiting for the first person to solve the mystery."

The Aldens looked at one another in surprise.

"Money?" echoed Benny.

Thomas nodded as Mrs. McGregor poured his tea. "I'm a lawyer, and one of my clients was a very wealthy businessman. Before he died, he came up with the idea for a mystery. Whoever solved the mystery would inherit a portion of his estate — that means a good chunk of his money."

"Who was he?" Benny wanted to know. "The businessman, I mean."

Thomas stirred cream into his tea. "My client wanted that to be kept a secret, Benny."

"You mean, until after the mystery's solved?" Mrs. McGregor looked puzzled.

"Before *and* after, Mrs. McGregor," answered Thomas. "The millionaire's name will *never* be revealed."

Henry scratched his head. "Why did he want to keep it a secret?"

Thomas said only, "I'm sure my client had his reasons."

Sam looked around at everyone. "The whole thing sounded kind of fishy to me. But Thomas swears that the invitation is for real." Sam was patting his shirt pockets. "Now, where did I put my glasses?" He glanced over at the Aldens. "Could someone read the invitation out loud for me?"

Jessie stood up. "Of course." She took the invitation from Sam, then began to read it aloud:

To Samuel Snow,
You are cordially invited to solve the mystery of the Spider's Clue.

In a separate envelope, you will find a series of clues that will lead you through Greenfield to a secret code word.

If you are the first to solve the mystery of the Spider's Clue and discover the secret code word, you will be the winner of an inheritance.

This code word must be given to Thomas Paintner, at the law firm of Paintner and Bradley, by July 12.

Good luck to one and all!

When she was finished, Jessie sank back against a cushion. She had never seen such a strange invitation before.

"There isn't much time to find the code word," Violet pointed out. "The twelfth of July is only one week away."

Thomas took a sip of his tea. "That's true," he said. "And there'll be others trying to solve the mystery, too."

"It seems odd," Henry said thoughtfully. "Why would the millionaire make a game out of giving away his money?"

Jessie was curious, too. "Why didn't he just name somebody in his will?"

"I bet the millionaire liked mysteries," Benny guessed, his eyes shining. "Maybe he wanted everyone to have some fun trying to solve one."

"You're a smart young man, Benny," said Thomas with a slow smile. "Not many people would've figured that out."

Benny smiled.

Sam put down his teacup and looked at each of the Aldens in turn. "I was wondering if you'd like to tackle this mystery for me," he said. "I'd try to solve it myself, but I can't get around much right now. It takes me a long time to walk anywhere."

The children didn't have to think about it. "We'd be happy to solve it for you," Henry said in an excited voice.

"Great!" Sam was pleased. "I was hoping you'd say that."

"Sam often tells me about the Alden adventures," said Thomas as he reached for another cookie. "And I love to hear about them. I quite enjoy a good mystery."

"Thomas is a big mystery fan," Sam told them. "Always has been."

Thomas laughed. "I've had a soft spot for mysteries ever since I was a kid," he confessed. "Even now, I like to hide a bit of candy somewhere in the house when my grandchildren come to visit. I make a list of codes and clues to help them track it down."

That sounded like fun to Benny. "Your grandchildren must really like visiting you."

"I think they do," said Thomas.

Suddenly Jessie had a thought. "What happens if nobody finds the code word?" she asked Thomas. "What happens to the inheritance?"

"According to my client's will, if no one solves the mystery, the money goes to his relatives."

Henry had a question, too. "Do you think the millionaire knew the people he sent invitations to?" he asked. "Or did he just pick their names out of the phone book?"

Thomas smiled mysteriously. "We may never know the answer to that."

The Aldens exchanged glances. Why was Sam's old friend being so vague?

As if reading their minds, Thomas quickly added, "I drew up the will, but my client didn't tell me much else. He requested that the invitations be sent out after his death, and his butler did that. I didn't even know Sam was on the mailing list until he called today. I know the code word, of course," he went on. "And I know that the first person to come up with it by July twelfth will inherit a nice sum of money. But I'm afraid that's all I know." Thomas glanced at his watch. "I don't like to rush off, but I do have another appointment."

"Yes, yes, of course," said Sam. "I appreciate your stopping by."

Thomas stood up. "You know, those cookies bring back a lot of memories. When we were kids, we used to eat cookies until they were coming out of our ears!" Thomas had a faraway look in his eyes. "We did everything together back then. Why, we were like the Three Musketeers — Sam and Simon and I. Do you remember the way little Pinky used to follow the three of us around, Sam? Whenever we — "

"The past is best forgotten!" Sam suddenly broke in, giving Thomas a hard look.

Everyone seemed surprised by Sam's harsh tone. Why was he getting so upset about the past? And who were Simon and Pinky?

Thomas looked as if he wanted to argue with his old friend, but he didn't. There was a strained silence until Mrs. McGregor finally spoke up.

"I'm glad you enjoyed the cookies, Thomas," she said, trying to change the subject. "They've always been a great favorite around the Alden house."

Thomas gave Mrs. McGregor a warm smile. Then he said good-bye and left.

Sam lay back on his pillows. He did not look one bit happy.

"You seem tired, Sam," Mrs. McGregor commented. "Perhaps we should be going, too."

Benny's eyes widened in alarm. "But what about the clues?" he cried. "We can't go before we open the other envelope!"

"Right you are," said Sam, stirring himself. He reached for the second envelope from the coffee table. "Would you like to open it for me, Benny?"

"Sure thing!" Benny jumped from the stool and took the envelope from Sam. Everyone held their breath as Benny opened it and pulled out a folded sheet of paper.

"Oh!" Benny exclaimed, his eyes widening as he unfolded the paper. "It's a poem!" He held it up for everyone to see.

"Would you like me to read it, Benny?" Violet asked. The youngest Alden was just learning to read.

Benny passed the poem to his sister.

Violet cleared her throat, then she read aloud:

> *When the sheep in the meadow*
> *And the cow in the corn*
> *Do a figure eight*
> *In the early morn,*
> *Look no further,*
> *For you will see*
> *The Spider's Clue*
> *In the hollow tree.*

Amazed, the Aldens sat in puzzled silence. Jessie looked at Henry. How would they ever figure out such a strange poem?

Sam seemed to know what they were thinking. "That's going to be a tough mystery to solve," he remarked. "You certainly have your work cut out for you."

Mrs. McGregor laughed. "If there's anything these children like, it's work!"

"We're good at figuring out clues," Benny told Sam. "We'll find that code word in no time." He turned to the others. "Right?"

"Yes," said Henry. Then he added honestly, "At least, we'll do our best."

Mrs. McGregor said, "Now you can relax, Sam. The mystery's in good hands. Besides, it's been ages since you've had any time away from your job."

Sam's eyes clouded. "Oh, I don't mind a bit of time to myself. But I do feel badly for my friends — the ones who rely on me. Some of them are getting older, you know. They can't get around much anymore. They really enjoy looking out their windows at the flowers and the trees." Sam shook his head sadly. "I try to keep their windows clean. Every week I do one or two houses for free. The homes where my older friends live, I mean."

"Maybe we could lend a hand," volunteered Henry.

"Of course," agreed Jessie, while Benny and Violet nodded eagerly.

Sam looked surprised — and pleased. "Would you?" he asked.

"We'd like to help," Violet said in her soft voice.

Sam looked at the children's eager faces. "Washing windows is hard work," he warned them.

"No problem!" Benny said. "We can handle it!"

"I just might take you up on that offer," Sam said, smiling for the first time. "I don't like to let folks down."

The Aldens looked at one another. They understood what Sam meant. Helping people always made them feel good, too.

"The houses aren't far from here." Sam scribbled the names and addresses on a piece of paper. "I know they'll appreciate your help."

Henry folded the paper that Sam handed to him. Then he carefully put the addresses in his pocket.

Jessie spoke up. "Do you mind if I make a copy of the Spider's Clue poem, Sam?"

Sam didn't mind at all. "Be my guest," he said.

Jessie tugged her small notebook and pencil from her pocket. While she copied the poem, the other Aldens helped Mrs. McGregor. They gathered up the glasses and saucers and teacups and took them into the kitchen to wash them. It wasn't until they were saying good-bye that the children remembered to give Sam their get-well card.

"Nobody's ever drawn a picture of me before," Sam told them, taking a long look at the card. "And a poem, too! I can't believe it."

Mrs. McGregor smiled. "Well, there's a first time for everything."

Sam tucked the get-well card into his shirt pocket. "This one is a keeper!" he said in a choked voice.

Violet was afraid Sam might get lonely all by himself. "We'll stop by every day," she promised. "And we'll keep you up to date on the mystery."

"I'd like that," Sam told her.

Jessie was worried about Sam, too. There was such a sad note in his voice. But she didn't know what to say to make him feel better, so she just stared out the window. Her eyes suddenly widened when she caught a glimpse of movement outside.

Was it just her imagination? Or was the same man still watching Sam's house from behind the trees?

CHAPTER 3

A Needle in a Haystack

"Guess what, Grandfather?" Benny was bursting with news at dinner that night.

James Alden was helping himself to some of Mrs. McGregor's creamed chicken. He looked puzzled, but only for a moment. "I bet you found a mystery to solve," he said, turning to his youngest grandson. "Am I right?"

Benny's mouth dropped open. "How did you know?"

Grandfather chuckled. "Because my grandchildren attract mysteries like a magnet attracts iron."

At that, the four Alden children couldn't help laughing. They went on to tell Grandfather everything that had happened when they went to visit Sam. When they were finished, their grandfather said, "Sam's right. You *do* have your work cut out for you."

"That's for sure," said Jessie. She passed the hot biscuits to Violet. "Especially when the clues are in such a strange poem." Jessie had the oddest feeling she'd heard the first few lines of that poem somewhere before. But she couldn't quite put her finger on where it was.

Violet sighed. "We only have one week to find the secret code word for Sam."

"That doesn't give you much time, does it?" said Grandfather.

Violet shook her head as she buttered a biscuit. "It sure doesn't."

"And don't forget," Henry reminded them. "There'll be other people in Greenfield trying to find it, too."

The Aldens looked at one another — they were all thinking the same thing. The hollow tree could be anywhere. Where would they start?

"There's a street map of Greenfield in my study," Grandfather suggested. "If you think it might help, I'll get it out for you after dinner."

That did seem like a good idea. "Thank you, Grandfather," said Violet. "A street map will help a lot."

By the time they were having dessert, Henry was deep in thought. After taking a bite of his apple pie, he said, "It's a funny coincidence that an old friend of Sam's is handling the millionaire's estate."

Jessie didn't think it was strange at all. "Almost everyone in town is a friend of Sam's," she reminded him.

Benny agreed. "He's lived here all his life."

"Not quite," corrected Grandfather. "Sam was born in Greenfield and he went to school here for a number of years. But the Snow family moved away after Sam's mother died. That's when his father decided to run the family business in Boston."

Henry was surprised to hear this. "I thought Sam had always lived in Greenfield."

Grandfather shook his head. "Sam and his brother were teenagers when they moved away. After they finished school in Boston, they went to work in the family business, too. Just like their father. But I think Sam always missed small-town life. After his father passed away, Sam gave up his job at Snow Carpets. That's when he moved back to Greenfield. He's been washing windows for a living ever since."

Violet said, "Sam loves washing windows. I can't imagine him doing anything else."

"I know what you mean," said Grandfather. "Of course, Sam would be rich if he'd stayed in Boston and run the family business with his brother. But his job in Greenfield makes him happy."

Benny grinned. "Pretty soon, Sam *will* be rich."

Violet clasped her hands together. "Oh,

this is so exciting," she said. "Let's start looking for the hollow tree first thing in the morning."

The others were quick to agree. They could hardly wait for tomorrow.

After breakfast the next morning, the children set to work making a picnic lunch to take along on their search for the hollow tree.

Jessie got out the bread, egg salad, lettuce, and pickles. Violet took apples from the crisper. Benny found paper plates and napkins. Henry filled a thermos with pink lemonade.

Jessie loaded everything into her backpack. "Let's take a look at Grandfather's map before we set out," she suggested.

The four Aldens and Watch hurried out to the boxcar.

"This is a wonderful street map," Henry said, unfolding it over the blue cloth that covered the table. "It even shows the small lanes and alleyways in town."

"Where should we start?" Benny asked.

"Well, we have a few choices," said Jessie. The others watched as she traced her finger along the map. "We can start downtown on Main Street . . . or over here in the Morningside neighborhood . . . or we can search the Greenfield College area first." Jessie was the best map reader in the family. She always knew how to get where they were going.

Nobody said anything for a moment. Then Violet drew in her breath as a sudden thought came to her.

"The poem!" she cried.

Everyone looked at her. "What about it?"

"It gives us a clue where to begin!" Violet's voice rose with excitement as she recited: "*When the sheep in the meadow/ And the cow in the corn/ Do a figure eight/ In the early morn.*"

Henry snapped his fingers in sudden understanding. "In the early morn — the Morningside neighborhood!"

"Wow!" Benny was excited. "We figured out the first clue already."

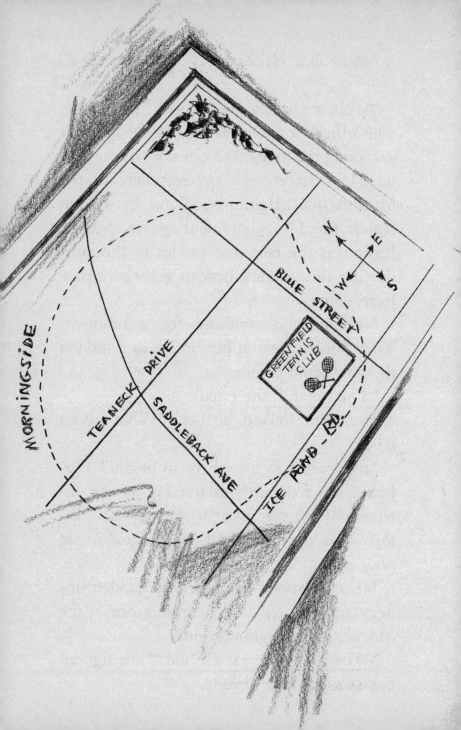

"That was good detective work, Violet," praised Jessie.

"Thanks." Violet was bending over the map again. "I like the Morningside neighborhood. The streets have such interesting names."

Jessie was studying the map, too. "I was thinking we could start on Teaneck Drive, then go over to Saddleback Avenue. After that, we can follow Ice Pond Road past the Greenfield Tennis Club and up as far as Blue Street. If we have time, we can even loop around and cover all the back lanes." Jessie looked up at the others. "How does that sound?"

Everyone thought it sounded just fine. Henry folded the map and tucked it into his back pocket.

While Jessie put her backpack and the Frisbee in the basket of her bike, Watch looked up at her, wagging his tail.

"Sorry, Watch," Jessie said. She knelt down and gave the little black-and-white dog a hug. "You can't come with us this time. We'll be riding our bikes."

Benny petted Watch softly on the head. "You can come with us later," he promised, "when we visit Sam."

A few minutes later, the Aldens were pedaling along the peaceful streets of Greenfield.

"Keep your eyes open for a hollow tree!" Henry reminded them.

The Aldens kept their eyes open. They rode up and down many streets of the Morningside neighborhood. But by noon they still hadn't caught even a glimpse of a hollow tree. When they stopped their bikes on Ice Pond Road to wait for a light to change, Benny spoke up.

"Is it time to eat yet?" he asked hopefully.

Henry glanced at his watch. "Close enough. I'm ready for a break."

"I second that!" Violet said, and Jessie nodded.

Before too long, Henry, Jessie, Violet, and Benny were sitting cross-legged on the lawn of the Greenfield Tennis Club. "What a perfect day for a picnic," Jessie said as she passed around the paper plates and napkins.

Benny sighed. "It's not a perfect day for solving a mystery." He held out his special cup as Violet poured the lemonade. It was the cracked pink cup he had found when they were living in the boxcar.

"We can't give up," Violet told him.

"That's true," said Henry as Jessie handed him an egg salad sandwich. "But at this rate, we'll never solve the mystery in a week."

"I know," Jessie agreed. "It'll take us forever to search every street in town. We haven't even finished the Morningside neighborhood yet."

No one said anything as they ate their sandwiches and pickles. There was nothing to say. What else could they do except ride up and down the streets? They couldn't think of any other way to find the hollow tree.

After lunch, Jessie pulled her notebook from her back pocket. While the other Aldens played Frisbee nearby, she reread the Spider's Clue poem. Once, twice, three times. Something was still puzzling her about the first few lines of the poem. She couldn't shake the feeling that she'd heard the words somewhere before. She was still trying to sort out her thoughts when her sister and brothers sat down again.

Benny crunched into an apple. "There sure are a lot of trees in Greenfield," he said, still thinking about the mystery.

Violet nodded. "Especially here in the Morningside neighborhood."

"Looking for a hollow tree in *this* neighborhood," said Benny, "is like . . . like — "

Henry smiled over at his brother. "Like looking for a needle in a haystack?"

"That's just what it's like," exclaimed Benny. "It's like looking for a needle in a haystack!"

Jessie looked at Benny in surprise. A funny look came over her face. Then she clapped her hands.

"Benny!" she exclaimed. "That's it!"

"What?" said Benny.

"I knew there was something familiar about the first few lines," she told them.

"The part about the sheep in the meadow and the cow in the corn, I mean."

The others stared at Jessie. They looked totally confused.

"When Benny mentioned a haystack," Jessie explained, "something just clicked. Those first few lines of the poem are from a nursery rhyme!"

"What nursery rhyme?" asked Henry.

Jessie shrugged. "I don't know," she admitted. "I can't really remember how it goes. But it says something about a cow and a sheep and a haystack."

"Let's find out about it," suggested Violet. "It might be an important clue."

"How will we find out?" asked Benny.

"We can look through some books at the library," Violet told them. "The ones with Mother Goose nursery rhymes in them."

The Aldens all decided it was a good idea. After cleaning up and making sure they hadn't left any litter, the children wheeled their bikes back onto the road and set off again.

Outside the Greenfield Public Library, Jessie said, "I hope this isn't a wild-goose chase."

"It's not." Benny grinned as they propped their bikes against some trees. "It's a *Mother* Goose chase!"

They all laughed at Benny's joke. Then Jessie suddenly stopped laughing. She looked around uneasily.

"What is it?" asked Henry.

"I'm not sure," said Jessie. "I just had the strangest feeling we were being watched."

The Aldens all stopped and looked behind them. But they didn't see anybody suspicious.

"Maybe somebody's hiding behind a tree," whispered Benny, sounding a little uneasy.

Jessie put an arm around Benny's shoulder. "I'm sure nobody's hiding, Benny," she said, not wanting her younger brother to worry. But she wasn't really sure at all.

CHAPTER 4

Wild-Goose Chase?

"Uh-oh!" said Benny. He paused as they entered the library. "We didn't bring our library cards."

"That's okay, Benny," Henry told him. "We can look through some books right here. We don't need a card for that."

The lady behind the information desk looked up. When she recognized the Aldens, she smiled and waved. The children were regular visitors to the library.

Jessie led the way to a long table in the middle of the room with a row of comput-

45

ers on it. "Let's browse through the computer catalog," she said quietly. "We can do a subject search for any books with nursery rhymes in them."

"Sounds good," said Henry.

It wasn't long before Jessie had found eight titles. In no time at all, they were able to locate the books in the children's section.

As they claimed an empty table by the window, Jessie reminded everyone, "We're looking for a nursery rhyme about a sheep and a cow and a — "

"Haystack," finished Benny, taking a seat next to Violet.

"Right," said Jessie, and she sat down beside Henry.

Benny opened a book. Then a frown crossed his round face.

Violet pulled her chair closer to her younger brother. "Why don't we work together," she suggested. She knew Benny would have trouble with the harder words.

Benny looked relieved. "Two heads are better than one," he whispered. "Right?"

Violet smiled. "That's just what I was thinking."

They hadn't been there very long before Jessie spotted a silver-haired man across the room. He was wearing faded jeans and a black T-shirt. Although his back was to them, he looked familiar.

Just then the man turned around. He stared right at Jessie, then he turned on his heel and hurried away. At that moment Jessie realized where she'd seen him before — he was the man who'd ducked behind the trees the other day!

Jessie tried to collect her thoughts. Why had the mystery man disappeared so quickly again? Had he followed them to the library?

The other Aldens still had their heads bent over their books, so Jessie decided not to say anything. She didn't want to frighten the younger children. After taking a long and careful look around, she breathed a sigh of relief. The man was nowhere to be seen.

Although she kept glancing over her shoulder, Jessie returned her attention to the nursery rhymes. A short time later, Violet and Benny found a rhyme with a cow in it. But the cow was jumping over the moon. And there wasn't any mention of sheep or haystacks. Then Henry showed them one about Little Bo Peep losing her sheep, but that wasn't right, either.

"Maybe I was wrong," Jessie whispered. "Maybe those lines weren't from a nursery rhyme."

Henry suddenly looked up. "You weren't wrong," he said. "Listen to this." He began to read quietly from the book.

> *Little Boy Blue,*
> *Come blow your horn.*
> *The sheep's in the meadow,*
> *The cow's in the corn;*
> *But where is the boy*
> *Who looks after the sheep?*
> *He's under a haystack,*
> *Fast asleep.*

"Hooray!" Benny cried, almost shouting. Then he clamped a hand over his mouth.

He had forgotten where he was for a moment.

"You were right after all, Jessie," Violet whispered, looking at her sister with admiration.

Jessie agreed that they'd found another piece of the puzzle. But where did it fit into the mystery?

Henry didn't know, either. "But I have a feeling," he said, "that if we can figure out what this Little Boy Blue clue is trying to tell us, then we'll know where to find the hollow tree."

Jessie thought about this for a minute. Then she nodded. "I think you're right, Henry."

Outside, Benny said, "I can't wait to tell Sam about this!"

"Let's tell him right now," suggested Violet, and the others nodded.

As they rode their bikes back through town, Henry noticed that Jessie was unusually quiet. He could see something was troubling her. "Is anything wrong?" he asked.

Jessie slowed her bike to a stop at a red

light. When she was sure the younger children were out of earshot, she told him about seeing the mystery man again.

"Are you sure it was the same man?" he asked.

"I can't be certain," admitted Jessie. "But I think so."

"You might be right, Jessie," Henry said thoughtfully. "But even if it was the same man, it could just be a coincidence that he happened to be at the library, too."

Jessie had to agree Henry had a point. "Maybe I *am* making too much of this. I suppose it could be a coincidence." But there was a small part of her that didn't believe it for a minute.

"Watch is a good buddy of mine," Sam said when the Aldens arrived with their dog. "Feel free to bring him along with you anytime."

At the sound of his name, Watch ran over to the couch where Sam was resting. The little dog jumped up and began to lick Sam's face.

Sam laughed as he scratched Watch between the ears. "What'd I tell you?" he said, looking over at the Aldens.

"Watch always likes coming here," said Henry.

Benny was bouncing up and down in his chair. "Guess what." He couldn't wait to tell Sam all about their day. "We figured out two clues already!"

"Did you really?" Sam asked, surprised to hear this.

The children took turns telling Sam all that had happened. Henry finished by saying, "The first few lines really were from a nursery rhyme. The one about Little Boy Blue."

"What . . . ?" Sam looked startled. For a moment, he just stared off into space as if in a trance.

Henry and Jessie exchanged glances. Why was Sam surprised by the nursery rhyme?

"Is anything wrong, Sam?" Violet asked.

Sam didn't answer.

"Sam?" Jessie asked.

Suddenly Sam jerked his head around. "Oh!" He seemed to have forgotten for a moment that he had company. "I'm sorry. I . . . I was lost in thought."

"Is everything okay?" Henry wondered.

Sam didn't answer right away. He had a faraway look in his eye. "Everything's fine," he said at last. "I just couldn't help remembering something. You see, that was my brother's favorite nursery rhyme. When he was small, I mean. That's how Simon got the nickname Blue." Sam smoothed his droopy mustache. "We all had colors for nicknames back then. Everybody called me Red, and Thomas was Brown. And then of course there was Pinky." Sam's voice had dropped so low, the Aldens could hardly hear him.

"Was Pinky your dog?" asked Benny.

"I don't let the past bother me anymore," said Sam as if he hadn't even heard Benny's question. "No point in crying over spilled milk."

"Oh," said Benny, still not sure who Pinky was.

Violet felt awful. It was plain that the past *did* bother Sam. Their visit was supposed to cheer him up. Instead, Sam's eyes were suddenly filled with sadness.

The children tried to change the subject. They asked Sam about washing windows instead, and he gave them some tips. By the time the Aldens were ready to leave, he was his usual cheery self again.

"I've got a hunch," he told them, "if you can figure out that Little Boy Blue clue, it'll lead you right to the hollow tree."

Jessie nodded. "That's what we thought, too."

But outside, Violet said, "It's a very strange clue. How are we ever going to figure it out?"

The other Aldens looked at one another. Nobody had an answer for that question.

CHAPTER 5

The Search Continues

"The millionaire sure left hard clues," Benny said the next morning.

The Aldens were standing on the front lawn of Mrs. Spencer's house. They had arrived to wash the outside of her windows. Just moments before, the elderly owner had come out to greet the children before going back inside the house.

"I wonder who he was," Benny went on. "The mysterious millionaire, I mean."

Henry turned on the hose. "There's no

way of knowing," he said as he filled the buckets with water.

Jessie added cleaning solution to the water. "It's funny that he wanted to keep his identity such a secret."

"We know one thing for sure," said Benny. "The millionaire was somebody who liked mysteries."

Violet nodded. "And he was good at making them up, too."

"But we're even better at solving them!" Benny was quick to remind them.

Jessie laughed. "I wonder just how good we are at washing windows."

"There's only one way to find out," said Henry.

With that, everyone grabbed a rag and set to work. Henry leaned the ladder against the house and climbed up to reach the top windows. Jessie, Violet, and Benny tackled the lower windows. While they worked, the children were each lost in thought about the mysterious millionaire and his strange clues.

"You really ought to take a break, children," a voice called out to them some time later. "If you're interested, I have some cold apple cider."

Violet turned to see Mrs. Spencer poking her head out of an opened window. Wisps of snowy-white hair fluttered in the breeze.

"Apple cider sounds great, Mrs. Spencer," Violet called back to her, while Benny let out a cheer. The four children had been working hard all morning and were ready for a break.

Henry stepped down from the ladder. "I guess we're done here anyway," he said. The Aldens stood back to admire their work.

"We did a good job," Benny said proudly, and the others agreed.

Inside, Mrs. Spencer poured apple cider into tall glasses while Henry, Jessie, Violet, and Benny sat around the table in her cheery little kitchen.

"What dear children you are!" said Mrs. Spencer, smiling over at them. As she sat down, she reached into her pocket and pulled out some dollar bills. "I want to give you a little something for — "

Jessie shook her head firmly. "Please put your money away, Mrs. Spencer."

"You deserve a reward for your hard work," insisted Mrs. Spencer.

"Grandfather says hard work is its own reward," Violet told her quietly.

Mrs. Spencer hesitated for a moment. Then she tucked the money into her pocket again. "Your grandfather is a wise man," she said. "And a lucky one, too."

Benny looked puzzled. "Lucky?"

"He's very lucky indeed to have such wonderful grandchildren." Mrs. Spencer gave them a happy smile. "Just look at how the sun comes shining through those clean windows! Oh, I shall enjoy watching the birds even more now."

The children chatted happily with the elderly woman. She talked for a while about Sam and how good he'd always been to her. Later, when she got up to answer the phone, the Aldens cleared away the empty glasses, waved good-bye, and walked back outside.

"Mrs. Spencer is such a sweet lady, isn't she?" Violet said.

"You know what I think?" Benny piped up as he helped give the rags a good wringing-out. "I think this is why Sam washes windows."

"What do you mean, Benny?" asked Henry.

"I think he does it because he likes making people happy."

Jessie nodded. "Sam's always thinking of others." She hung the buckets over the handlebars of her bike. "I just hope we can solve the mystery for him."

"Oh, if only we could figure out that Little Boy Blue clue!" cried Violet. "I can't stop thinking about it."

"And we won't stop," Henry said firmly. "Not until we come up with an answer."

Everybody nodded except Benny.

"I'm too hungry to think," he said.

Henry laughed. "We get the hint, Benny. Let's go home and get something to eat."

It wasn't long before the Aldens were enjoying a delicious lunch of cheese sandwiches, Mrs. McGregor's homemade potato chips, and crisp apples.

"If we can't figure it out," Henry said, "we'll have to ride up and down the streets again." The children were still talking about the Little Boy Blue clue as they sat in the kitchen of their grandfather's big white house.

"You're right, Henry." Jessie poured Benny another glass of milk. "And that means going back to the Morningside neighborhood to hunt for the hollow tree. We didn't quite finish checking out all the streets."

Benny swallowed a bite of his sandwich. "We searched *most* of them, though," he reminded them. "We went all the way up Ice Pond Road almost as far as — " Benny stopped talking. He was suddenly staring wide-eyed at his brother and sisters.

"What is it?" asked Henry.

"We . . . we got almost as far as *Blue* Street!"

Henry, Jessie, and Violet looked at Benny in amazement. "Of course!" cried Jessie.

"The Little Boy Blue nursery rhyme's telling us to go to *Blue* Street!"

Henry gave his younger brother a big smile. "Great thinking, Benny!"

After they finished lunch, the children went out to the boxcar to study the map again.

"It's a very long street," observed Violet, pointing on the map to where Blue Street started and where it ended. "Any idea where we should begin?"

"I'm not sure," Jessie answered, without taking her gaze off the map. "But at least we've narrowed it down to just the one street — even if it is a long one."

Henry smiled a little and said, "I think we can narrow it down even more. I have a feeling we should be looking right about here." Henry put his finger on the map just where Blue Street crossed Ice Pond Road.

"Why do you say that, Henry?" Violet asked curiously.

"Remember how the Spider's Clue poem goes?" asked Henry. Then he began to recite: *"When the sheep in the meadow/ And the cow in the corn/ Do a figure eight/ In the early morn.*" Then he straightened up and looked over at his brother and sisters. "Does that remind you of anything? The part about the figure eight, I mean."

Jessie, Violet, and Benny thought hard for a minute. Then Jessie's face brightened as she suddenly caught on. "I do figure eights whenever I go skating!"

Henry nodded. "Exactly."

Benny was confused. "Jessie's a good skater, but what does that have to do with anything?"

Just then Violet said, "Oh!" She put one hand over her mouth in surprise. "I think I know what Henry means. Skaters can do figure eights on ice ponds!"

"Ice Pond Road!" cried Benny. "Come on!" He was already halfway out of the box-car. "Let's go check it out."

The Aldens set off for the Morningside neighborhood once again. In no time at all they reached the corner of Ice Pond Road and Blue Street. The children hopped off their bikes and took a good look around at

the four corners of the intersection. Their gaze took in a barbershop, a vacant lot overgrown with weeds, a bookstore, and a small restaurant with a pink awning.

But there wasn't a hollow tree anywhere in sight.

"I don't get it." Violet checked out the street signs again. "According to the clues, this should be the spot." She looked over at Henry. "Right?"

Henry nodded. "Has to be," he said.

"Then where's the hollow tree?" asked Benny.

Puzzled, they all looked at one another. Then Jessie shook her head.

"Something doesn't add up," she said. "Maybe we read the clues wrong."

"What now?" Benny wanted to know, his shoulders slumped with disappointment.

The Aldens looked at one another. They didn't know what to do.

CHAPTER 6

A Surprising Discovery

The Aldens refused to give up. The next day they went back to riding their bikes up and down the streets of Greenfield.

"We've been all over the Morningside neighborhood," Jessie pointed out as they sat on a bench in the town square. The children were taking another look at the map. "And we've checked every street downtown, too."

"What I can't figure out is why the clues lead right here," Violet said. She pointed on the map to where Blue Street and Ice Pond Road crossed.

"I vote we ride over and take another look around," said Benny. "Maybe we missed something."

The older children weren't sure about this. Still, it couldn't hurt to take another look.

Henry folded the map and tucked it into his back pocket. "I guess it's possible we overlooked some kind of clue."

The four Aldens walked across the brick-paved square to where they'd parked their bikes in a lot. They were deep in thought when a voice raised in argument caught their attention.

"I'm warning you! You'll be sorry if you do."

The Aldens turned to see a silver-haired man standing at a pay phone making a call. Although his back was toward them, Jessie recognized the mystery man immediately. She ducked out of sight behind a parked car and motioned to the others to do the same.

Now the man was almost shouting. "We agreed to see this mystery through to the end! I expect you to keep your word." The man suddenly hung up the phone, then turned and walked away, looking upset.

After peering all around, Benny said, "I think the coast is clear."

Jessie turned to Henry as they came out from their hiding place. "That was the same man I saw across from Sam's house, and then again at the library."

Henry looked at Jessie in surprise. "Maybe something *is* going on."

"Who is he?" Benny wanted to know.

"I don't have a clue who that man is," Jessie answered. "But I know he's up to something."

"He mentioned a mystery," Violet pointed out. "Do you think he was talking about the mystery of the Spider's Clue?"

"I'm sure of it," answered Jessie.

Henry frowned. "That can only mean one thing."

Jessie looked at him. "What?"

"That he got an invitation in the mail, too."

"Do you really think so?"

Henry nodded. "Why else would he be talking about the mystery?"

Jessie was certain Henry was right. "That would explain his interest in Sam," she said thoughtfully. "And maybe it explains his interest in us, too. He's probably trying to find out how much we know."

Violet walked her bike beside Jessie. "I bet he's hoping we'll lead him right to the code word."

"We'd better keep an eye on him from now on," suggested Henry.

"And we'd better find the code word fast!" Benny added.

When they arrived at the corner of Blue Street and Ice Pond Road, the children made a careful search of the area. But once again, they found nothing that would help.

"Looks like we struck out again," Henry said.

Jessie looked at her watch. "It's almost noon," she pointed out. "Why don't we talk about this over lunch?"

The children decided to eat at the restaurant on the corner of Blue Street and Ice Pond Road. They waited for the light to change, then crossed the street. After leaving their bikes under the pink awning by the window, they went inside.

The restaurant was bright and cheery. It had a pink-and-white-tiled floor. There were pink leather booths along one side of the room and wooden stools with comfortable pink cushions at a counter on the other side. Pink roses in pretty vases had been placed on every table. And a collection of plants in pink ceramic pots hung in the window of a sunny little alcove.

"Somebody sure likes pink," Benny remarked as he looked around. Suddenly he spotted a familiar face. "Look! Isn't that Thomas?"

Sure enough, Thomas Paintner was sitting at a booth in the corner. There was a young woman in a pale yellow business suit sitting with him. She was wearing reading glasses, and her dark hair was pulled back from her face with a shiny gold clip.

When Thomas saw the Aldens, he waved

them over. "It's good to see you again!" he said with a friendly smile. Then he introduced them to his legal assistant, Melissa Campbell.

The children nodded politely and said hello, but the young woman barely looked at them. She was busy making notes in the margins of some papers.

"Any luck with Sam's mystery?" Thomas wanted to know.

His legal assistant suddenly glanced up.

"No luck yet," said Henry.

"Oh," said Thomas. "Too bad." He sounded disappointed.

"But we'll figure it out," put in Benny. "Just wait and see."

Melissa Campbell smiled with amusement. "Pretending to be detectives, are you?"

"We're not pretending!" Benny said indignantly. "We've solved lots of mysteries!"

Melissa gave the Aldens a sharp look. "Oh, I'm sure you've solved *hundreds* of them."

Benny could feel his face turning bright red. He wasn't used to anyone making fun of him. "We haven't solved hundreds," he said, "but . . . but . . ." His voice trailed away. He didn't know what to say.

Henry squared his shoulders. "We *have* solved quite a few," he said, looking Melissa straight in the eye.

Thomas spoke up. "Actually, these kids are real pros," he told his assistant. "They have a real talent for figuring out clues."

Melissa rolled her eyes. "I bet they even have their own office with a big sign out front."

Jessie was ready with an answer. "Our boxcar is all the office we need."

"We found it in the woods," Benny added proudly. "And now the boxcar's in our backyard."

"How very . . . unusual," said Melissa. Then she turned away and went back to her paperwork.

"Feel free to stop by my office anytime." Thomas handed his business card to Henry. "I'm on Elm Street," he added. "And I'm never too busy for a visit from the Aldens."

Henry tucked the card into his shirt pocket as everyone said good-bye.

"That lady wasn't very nice," whispered Benny as the children made their way toward an empty booth. "Why doesn't she believe we solve mysteries?"

"Some grown-ups are like that," Henry said as they settled into a booth. "They don't realize kids can figure things out for themselves."

"Did you notice how Melissa ignored us at first?" Violet said after a moment's thought. "Until Thomas mentioned the mystery, that is. Then she was suddenly very interested." Violet frowned. "Don't you think that was odd?"

Henry shrugged. "I guess she thought it was funny."

But Violet thought there was more to it than that. She had a hunch Melissa Campbell had taken a special interest in them for some reason. But why?

As they looked over the menus carefully, they forgot all about Thomas and his assistant. Before long, an older woman in high

heels came over to take their orders. Henry asked for a grilled cheese sandwich with coleslaw and milk. So did everyone else.

The waitress suddenly let out a long sigh. "These high-heeled shoes are killing me," she confided. "It's impossible to walk in these things."

The Aldens looked over at her. The waitress was dressed all in pink. There were even pink bows on her high-heeled shoes, and her long fingernails flashed with pink nail polish.

Although Benny was trying not to stare, the waitress caught his look.

"It makes me feel cheery to wear pink," she said, smiling. "Pink's my favorite color."

Violet spoke up shyly. "Purple's my favorite color."

A warm smile spread across the woman's face. "That must be why you're wearing a purple ribbon in your hair!" She looked thoughtfully at the Aldens. "You're friends of Sam Snow, aren't you?" When the children stared at her in surprise, she gave them a wink. "I heard you mention Sam. I'm afraid you can't help overhearing things when you're a waitress. It goes with the territory."

"Are you a friend of Sam's, too?" Violet asked.

"Yes, Sam and I have known each other for years." The waitress held out her hand. "My name's Rose Hill. I own this little restaurant."

"It's nice to meet you," said Violet, shaking hands. "I'm Violet Alden. And this is my sister, Jessie, and my brothers, Henry and Benny."

As everyone shook hands, Rose said, "Welcome to the Hollow Tree!"

The Aldens all looked at one another in disbelief. "Did . . . did you just call this place the 'Hollow Tree'?" Benny asked, astonished.

"That's right," replied Rose. Then she sighed. "I'm not surprised you didn't know the name of my restaurant. The sign on the awning out front is badly faded." She tucked her notepad into her apron pocket. "I'm hoping to have some money soon to fix up this old place. By the way, if you see Sam," she added, "tell him I'll be taking him out for lunch tomorrow. And I won't be taking no for an answer!" With that, she teetered away in her high heels.

The children were still so shocked by what they'd heard, they couldn't speak for a moment. Then Jessie said, "I can't believe it! We're actually sitting in the Hollow Tree."

Henry nodded. "Good thing we decided to stop for a bite to eat!"

"So," reasoned Violet, "if this place is the Hollow Tree, then the Spider's Clue must be around here somewhere."

"But where?" Benny said thoughtfully.

The children kept craning their necks and peering around the room over lunch. But they weren't sure what they were looking for. What kind of clue *was* the Spider's Clue?

"What do we do now?" asked Benny as he finished the last bite of his sandwich.

"Wash windows," answered Henry. He

wiped his mouth with a napkin. "We promised Mr. Arnold, remember?"

The four Aldens were anxious to work on the mystery, but they didn't want to break a promise. Mr. Arnold was one of the senior citizens on Sam's list.

Violet borrowed Jessie's notebook. She made a quick sketch of the room to study later. Then the children paid their bill and hurried away.

Nobody noticed that though Thomas Paintner had left the restaurant, Melissa Campbell still sat at the table, waiting and watching the Aldens through narrowed eyes.

CHAPTER 7

Along Came a Spider!

"Why don't we visit Sam on our way home," suggested Henry.

The four Aldens had worked hard all afternoon washing the windows of Mr. Arnold's red brick house. Now they were pedaling back along the streets of Greenfield, with buckets hung over their handlebars.

Benny was quick to agree with his older brother. "Sam sure will be surprised when we tell him about the Hollow Tree Restaurant."

"Speaking of Sam," said Violet, who was riding right beside Benny, "why don't we stop at the nursery on our way and get him a plant."

Jessie nodded. "It *would* be a nice surprise."

"That's a great idea, Violet," said Henry, and the others agreed.

Benny was all smiles. "Sam will have *two* surprises in one day!"

The Greenfield Nursery was overflowing with plants. There were plants in hanging baskets and in flower boxes and in colorful ceramic pots. The children had trouble making up their minds.

"Don't forget," Benny reminded them, "Sam doesn't have much room. His tables are covered with get-well cards."

"Good point," said Jessie. "Maybe we should get him a plant in a hanging basket."

Violet tilted her head back and looked up. "What about this one?"

The others followed her gaze to a plant in a pretty wicker basket. Beautiful green leaves billowed over the sides of the basket, with several wiry stems dangling low. Along the ends of the stems, smaller plants were growing.

Henry nodded. "I like it," he said simply.

"Me, too," added Benny.

Jessie smiled. "It's different from all the others. I think it's just right for Sam."

"It's hard to choose, isn't it?" said a voice behind them, and the children turned around quickly in surprise.

A woman with gray streaks in her dark hair smiled at them. She was wearing blue overalls with the words GREENFIELD NURS-ERY embroidered across the front.

"Hi, Adella!" cried Benny. "Remember us?"

"Of course! You're the children who bought the Japanese maple tree."

Jessie nodded. "You have a good memory." For their grandfather's birthday, the Aldens had given him a tree with beautiful red leaves.

"Now we're getting a present for somebody else," put in Benny. "This time, it's for Sam the Window Man."

"Oh!" Adella smiled more broadly. "Well, in that case, it's half price. Anything in the nursery!"

"Thank you," said Henry. Then he pointed. "That's the one we want."

Adella nodded. "Ah, you like the Chlorophytum, do you?"

Benny made a face. "The Chloro-*what*?"

Adella laughed. "Chlorophytum," she said again. "At least that's the scientific name for it."

Jessie pulled her notebook and pencil from her back pocket. She quickly scribbled down the name of the plant and the instructions for its care. She wanted Sam to have all the right information.

"Of course, you'll need a hook to hang it on," added Adella. "We have a nice selection here." She gestured to an assortment of hooks and then moved away to help another customer.

"Even Adella knows Sam," Benny remarked. "No wonder he got so many get-well cards. Right, Violet?"

But Violet didn't answer. Something had caught her attention.

Benny followed her gaze to where a young man with sandy-colored hair was watering some plants. He was wearing overalls just like Adella's, and he was having a heated discussion with a woman dressed in pale yellow.

"Isn't that Melissa Campbell?" Violet whispered.

Benny wasn't too sure about that. "Maybe," he said, trying to keep his voice low. The woman was half hidden by a potted fir tree.

The children didn't mean to eavesdrop. But from where they were standing, they couldn't help overhearing bits and pieces of the conversation.

"I'm telling you, it won't work." The young man sounded upset.

"Oh, this is turning into a great day!" the woman shot back, though it was plain from her voice that it wasn't turning into a great day at all. "I suppose I'll have to do it myself!"

"Look, I just don't think we can pull it off."

The woman suddenly clicked her tongue. "Now listen to me, Ray! You want to get rid of your debts, don't you? And I want to get as far away from this boring town as possible! This is our one big chance — and you'd better not mess it up!"

With that, the woman stomped away.

Violet and Benny watched closely until she disappeared out the door. There was no doubt about it. The woman was Melissa Campbell.

Benny's eyes were wide. "Did you hear that?"

Just then, the sandy-haired man came storming down the aisle. He almost bumped right into Benny. Whirling around on his heel, he snapped at them, "You kids shouldn't be underfoot! Don't you have better things to do than stand around here?"

Then he stalked off.

"What was that all about?" Henry wanted to know.

Benny shrugged. "I didn't mean to get underfoot," he said in a small voice.

Jessie put an arm around him. "Don't worry, Benny," she said, trying to comfort him. "You didn't do anything wrong."

Henry frowned. "I wonder what Melissa meant about one big chance."

"I think they're up to no good," said Benny.

"We can't be sure, Benny," Violet told him.

"Well, they're up to something!" he insisted.

Henry nodded. "There seem to be a lot of strange things going on in Greenfield lately."

"Thanks, kids. A plant is just what this room needs," said Sam as Henry fastened the hook to the living room ceiling.

Jessie consulted her notebook. "It's a Chlorophytum. And it needs lots of water."

Sam thought for a moment. "I don't

know a whole lot about plants," he admitted, "but I think there's a more common name for that particular one." He scratched his head. "I just can't remember what it is."

After making sure the hook was secure, Henry carefully hung the basket by the window.

Sam looked around gratefully at the Aldens. "I was just about to whip up something for dinner. I'd love a bit of company if you'd like to join me."

"We *would* like to stay," Jessie said, speaking for them all, "but why don't you let us get dinner ready."

Sam thought about this for a moment. "Well . . . if you're certain it's not too much trouble."

The Aldens were eager to do whatever they could for Sam. "It's no trouble at all," said Henry.

While Sam relaxed, the children hurried off to the kitchen. After letting Mrs. McGregor know about their change of plans, they washed their hands and set to work. They found leftover chicken in the refrigerator, along with fresh fruits and vegetables. There was a large box of rice in the cupboard.

"How about a stir-fry?" suggested Jessie, and the others agreed.

While she waited for the water to boil for the rice, Jessie cut the chicken into bite-sized pieces. Henry sliced up mushrooms, green peppers, onions, and celery. Violet and Benny chopped bananas and apples for a fruit salad.

The youngest Alden was still thinking about the mystery. He paused as he spooned fruit salad into bowls. "I wonder what kind of clue a spider would leave."

Henry stirred the chicken and vegetables together in a pan on the stove. "That's a good question, Benny." He added a dash of soy sauce to the stir-fry. "One thing's for sure: The Spider's Clue is somewhere inside the Hollow Tree Restaurant."

When they were all seated at the table, Sam took a bite of the stir-fry and nodded approvingly.

"Tastes just as good as it smells," he said.

Violet looked relieved. "We were hoping you'd like it."

Taking turns, the children told Sam all about their day. "The clues led us to the corner of Blue Street and Ice Pond Road," said Jessie. She took a sip of milk. "We thought we'd struck out until we stopped for lunch at the — "

"Hollow Tree Restaurant!" finished Benny.

Sam shook his head in disbelief. "I should have thought of that myself. After all, I stop in there all the time. There really was a hollow tree there once, you know. In fact, that's how the restaurant got its name."

The Aldens looked at him in surprise.

"On that very spot?" asked Henry.

With a sweep of his hand, Sam said, "The whole Morningside area was just farmland back then. All open fields and meadows. When we were kids, my brother and I used to play hockey there with Thomas on a pond that would freeze over every winter."

"No wonder it's called Ice Pond Road," Henry realized.

"My brother, Simon, would stash our

lunches in the hollow tree. When we got hungry, we'd just skate over and grab something to eat. Guess that's why I remember it so well." Sam stopped talking and took a breath. "When I moved back to town years later, that whole area had been built up." His voice suddenly wavered. "I knew things would never be the same again."

When a frown crossed Sam's kind face, Violet couldn't help wondering why the past bothered him so much. But she didn't ask.

"I think that's the right place for the Chlorophytum," Jessie said, changing the subject. "By the window, I mean."

Violet smiled gratefully at her older sister. She could always count on Jessie to come to the rescue. "It does look nice there," Violet added.

"And I'll make sure it gets enough water," said Sam. He seemed relieved to be talking about something else.

After dinner, the Aldens cleared the table while Sam went into the living room to lie down.

"It's funny how the clues keep reminding Sam of the past," said Benny.

The others nodded. They'd noticed this, too.

Violet filled the sink with hot soapy water. "It really is strange," she said in a quiet voice. "Sam gets so unhappy whenever the past is mentioned."

"I just wish we could help." Jessie stacked plates on the counter.

Henry thought about that. "We can't help if we don't know what's wrong," he said.

"Why don't we ask," suggested Benny.

Henry shook his head as he put the leftover rice in the refrigerator. "Remember what happened when Thomas mentioned the past?"

"Sam didn't like it one bit," Benny recalled.

"Besides," Jessie added, "it's not really any of our business." She reached for a dish towel. "If Sam wants to tell us, he will."

The children finished quickly. In no time

at all, the table had been cleared, the dishes washed, and the kitchen counters wiped clean.

"As soon as I'm on the mend," Sam told them when they sat down again in the living room, "it'll be my turn to cook. I make a pretty good bowl of chili."

"It's a deal!" said Jessie. It made her smile to think of Sam bustling about again.

Benny was staring hard at the Chlorophytum. "That plant looks like a big green spider hanging from the ceiling," he said thoughtfully.

Violet studied the Chlorophytum. Benny was right. It really did look like a green spider.

Sam snapped his fingers. "Spider plant!" he exclaimed. "That's the name I couldn't remember. Chlorophytum's the scientific name, of course. But most folks just call it a spider plant."

Violet's brown eyes widened. "I think we should be paying another visit to the Hollow Tree."

"Oh!" cried Jessie, as she caught Violet's meaning. "Do you think one of the plants in the restaurant could be a spider plant?"

Henry answered first. "I'm sure of it! And that's just where we'll find the Spider's Clue." He sounded excited.

"Yippee!" cried Benny, clapping his hands.

"Unless I miss my guess," Sam put in, "you'll have this mystery wrapped up real soon."

But would it be soon enough? Tomorrow was the twelfth of July, the last day to solve the mystery. The Aldens were quickly running out of time.

CHAPTER 8

A Shadow in the Night

Watch growled softly.

Benny sat up in bed. "What's wrong, Watch?" he asked in a sleepy voice.

After a long day, the Aldens had sat up in the boxcar, talking about their mystery. But now it was the middle of the night and they were all in bed. The house was dark and quiet. Why was Watch barking?

"Grrr," Watch growled again. He began to scratch at the bedroom door.

Benny slid out of bed and padded across the room. He opened the door. Watch dashed out into the hall, then raced down the stairs, barking loudly.

Henry, Jessie, and Violet came out of their rooms.

"What's the matter with Watch?" Jessie wanted to know.

Before Benny could answer, Grandfather stepped out into the hall, pulling his bathrobe around him.

"What's all the fuss about?" he asked, flicking the light switch.

Benny blinked at the brightness. "I think Watch hears something outside."

"Let's go see what's wrong," said Grandfather.

Everyone followed James Alden downstairs. They found Watch in the kitchen, scratching at the back door.

Benny ran to the window and peered out into the night. Was that a shadow moving across the yard?

"Wait here," said Grandfather. "I'll take a look around." He took the flashlight down from the shelf so he could find his way in the dark.

"Be careful!" Violet called out in a worried voice.

Henry, Jessie, Violet, and Benny watched through the opened doorway as Grandfather's flashlight beam swept back and forth across the yard.

At that moment, Benny heard a car door slam shut. He looked up at Jessie. "Did you hear that?"

"Hear what?"

"I think the prowler just made his getaway," Benny told her.

Shaking her head, Jessie said, "I doubt there was a prowler here, Benny. Watch probably just heard a raccoon in the yard."

"Maybe," said Benny. But he didn't sound convinced.

A few minutes later, Grandfather came back inside, with Watch close on his heels.

Grandfather put the flashlight away in the cupboard. "I'm not sure what got Watch so upset," he said. "It's pretty quiet out there."

Henry nodded. "Watch seems fine now."

"Why don't we go back upstairs," suggested Grandfather. "Our warm beds are waiting for us."

Violet shivered in her pajamas. "Watch will keep an eye on things for us."

"That's why we call him Watch." Jessie laughed. "Right, Benny?"

But Benny didn't answer. He was peering out the window again. Somebody had been prowling around out there. He was sure of it.

"I didn't hear a thing," Mrs. McGregor told the Aldens the next morning. "Not even Watch barking."

"Just as well," said Grandfather as he sat down at the breakfast table. "It turned out to be a false alarm."

The Aldens' housekeeper was dishing up scrambled eggs. She smiled over at Benny. "Looks like somebody could use a little more sleep."

Benny covered his mouth as he yawned. Then he shook his head. "There's no time for sleep."

Grandfather stirred cream into his coffee.

"Oh, yes. Today is your last chance to find the secret code word, isn't it?"

Henry nodded. "If nobody finds it by the end of the day, the inheritance goes to the millionaire's relatives."

Grandfather took a bite of his bacon and chewed thoughtfully. Then he said, "This mystery certainly came along at exactly the right time for Sam, didn't it? Just when he can't work for a while — presto! — he suddenly has a chance to inherit money. It's really quite an amazing coincidence."

"I was hoping the mystery would perk Sam up a bit," added Mrs. McGregor. "But I'm afraid he still isn't himself. It's just because of his job, of course. Sam really misses his work."

But Violet didn't think that was all it was. She was sure something else was troubling Sam Snow.

"The mystery keeps stirring up sad memories for him," she told Mrs. McGregor.

"It *is* weird," put in Henry. "The clues seem to remind Sam of his brother. He gets a faraway look in his eye and — "

"He's not one bit happy anymore," finished Benny.

Grandfather nodded. "There's a reason for that."

The children turned to their grandfather in surprise.

"What is it, Grandfather?" asked Jessie.

James Alden put down his fork. "Long ago, when Sam Snow turned his back on the family business, it caused quite a rift between the two brothers."

Benny looked puzzled. "What's a rift?"

"It means they had a disagreement," explained Jessie.

"That's exactly right," said Grandfather. "I remember hearing about it at the time. Simon didn't want his brother to leave the family business. He thought Sam was making a big mistake. There was an argument, and some terrible things were said. When Sam walked out the door, it was the last time the two brothers saw — or spoke to — each other in almost forty years."

"Didn't they ever try to patch things up?" Violet wondered.

Grandfather thought for a moment, then shook his head. "No, I don't think they ever did. I guess they were both too proud. Neither of them wanted to make the first move."

"Sam must miss his brother so much," Violet said softly.

"And Pinky, too," Benny put in. "Pinky was Sam's dog. At least, I think he was. But I'm not sure."

Jessie sighed. "We have so many questions."

"And so few answers," said Henry.

After breakfast, Jessie raced away to get her notebook. The other Aldens waited for her beside their bikes. A few minutes later, she leaned out the door of the boxcar.

"It's gone!" she shouted.

In a flash, Henry, Violet, and Benny came running. Henry was the first to climb up the stump step and then into the boxcar. "What's gone?" he asked.

Jessie turned to her older brother. "I can't find my notebook."

"Are you sure you left it in the boxcar last night?" Henry wanted to make sure.

"Yes," said Jessie. "It was right here on the table." Now there was nothing left on the table except the blue cloth.

"I don't understand it," Henry said, looking around. "Even Grandfather's street map is missing. I'm positive I left it out here."

Violet looked around, too. "Jessie's notebook was beside Grandfather's map. They were both on the table. Remember? We were talking about the mystery while we were sitting right here in the boxcar last night."

Just then, Watch came running into the boxcar. He dropped something at Jessie's feet. Then the little dog looked up, wagging his tail.

Jessie bent down to examine what Watch had dropped.

"What is it, Jessie?" asked Benny.

"Looks like a broken heel from somebody's shoe."

"I bet the prowler broke a heel rushing

away in the dark last night," guessed Benny. "Watch is a good watchdog *and* a good detective!"

"You think there really *was* a prowler?" Violet asked in alarm.

Henry nodded firmly. "It looks like it — *someone* stole Jessie's notebook and Grandfather's map."

The other Aldens didn't like the sound of this. Why would a prowler steal Jessie's notebook and Grandfather's map? It had to be somebody who was tracking down the secret code word. And now that person knew as much about the mystery as they did!

Violet's eyes were huge. "My sketch of the Hollow Tree Restaurant was in there, too. Whoever the thief is, he'll know just where to look for the Spider's Clue."

"You mean *she'll* know just where to look," corrected Jessie. She held up the broken heel. "This is from a woman's high-heeled shoe."

"Come on!" Henry was already halfway

out the boxcar. "We've got to find that secret code word — before somebody else finds it first!"

As soon as the Alden children arrived at the Hollow Tree Restaurant, Rose hurried over to greet them. "We're packed with the breakfast crowd right now," she apologized. "You might have to wait a few minutes for a booth."

"Oh, that's no problem," said Jessie.

"Mind if we take a look at your plants while we're waiting?" asked Henry.

"Go right ahead! I take quite an interest in plants myself." Rose gave them all a smile before hurrying away.

"Notice something different about Rose?" Benny whispered to Jessie as they followed Henry over to the window in the little alcove.

"What do you mean?"

"She isn't wobbling all over the place today."

Jessie looked over her shoulder. Benny was right. The owner of the Hollow Tree

Restaurant was dashing from booth to booth. Rose Hill wasn't teetering on high heels anymore.

There was no time to think about it, though. Jessie turned her attention to the plants in pink ceramic pots that were hanging in the window. Each plant was different from the next. Some had velvety leaves, some had waxy leaves. Some had pink flowers, some had red flowers. Some had twisted stems, some had straight stems.

It was Benny who spotted the spider plant first. "Look!" he whispered. He pointed to one that looked just like Sam's.

Next to him, Jessie said, "Way to go, Benny!"

The four Aldens peered long and hard at the spider plant.

After a long silence, Violet said, "I don't get it."

"I don't, either," said Henry.

Jessie shook her head. "I don't see anything that looks like a clue."

But Benny saw something the others didn't.

"Look on the bottom of the pot!" he exclaimed. "I think it's a clue."

Sure enough, some kind of message had been painted in bright yellow on the bottom of the ceramic pot.

Violet clapped her hands together softly. "It's the Spider's Clue!"

"Oh, Benny!" Jessie said proudly. "What would we do without you?"

Henry read the words aloud: " '*A rose by any other name would smell as sweet.*' "

The youngest Alden scrunched up his face. "What does *that* mean?"

Henry explained, "It means that a rose would still smell nice, even if we called it something else. I think it's from a play by Shakespeare — *Romeo and Juliet.*"

"Oh." Benny thought about this for a moment. "You mean, even if we called it a stinkweed instead of a rose, it would still smell good?"

"That's right," said Henry, hiding a smile. "Even if we called it a stinkweed."

Just then, something caught Violet's eye. A young man was sitting at a booth nearby

reading a newspaper. He was wearing a blue baseball cap with the letters GN on the front. This man was peering over his paper, staring at the Aldens.

Violet leaned closer to the others. "Maybe we should go somewhere else to talk," she whispered, looking nervously over her shoulder.

"Aren't we getting something to eat?" Benny asked, making them all laugh.

"We just finished breakfast, Benny," Jessie reminded him.

Henry winked. "A Benny by any other name would still be hungry all the time," he joked, making them all laugh even harder.

"That's for sure!" agreed Benny.

A little later, the four Aldens were sitting under a tree at the Greenfield Tennis Club. They were thinking hard about the Spider's Clue when Violet suddenly spoke up.

"I still can't believe somebody stole your notebook, Jessie." Violet couldn't stop thinking about it. "And Grandfather's street map, too. Who would do such a thing?"

Henry had a thought. "Maybe that broken heel belongs to Rose Hill," he said. When he saw the look of surprise on everyone's faces, he added, "She was wearing high heels yesterday. But today she was just wearing sandals."

"That's true," said Jessie. She remembered Rose dashing from booth to booth.

"You don't really believe it was Rose, do you, Henry?" Violet liked Rose and hated to think of her prowling around in the night.

"Rose needs money to fix up her restaurant," Henry argued. "Remember? And she could've seen Jessie's notebook when you were making that sketch, Violet."

This got Jessie thinking. "Rose *did* admit she overhears things. I wonder if she heard us talking about the inheritance."

"What about Melissa Campbell?" Violet said after a moment's thought. "I still think it was odd that she ignored us until Thomas mentioned the mystery. Then she was all ears."

"We even told her about our boxcar," recalled Henry.

Jessie lowered her voice and looked serious. "The mystery man belongs at the top of our list of suspects," she said. "There's something very suspicious about him."

"But" — Benny looked doubtful — "the prowler was a woman."

"You're forgetting something," replied Jessie. "The mystery man was talking to somebody on the phone about the mystery."

"And it could've been a woman," Henry concluded.

Jessie sighed. "For all we know, half of Greenfield could be looking for the secret code word."

Violet glanced at her watch. "We really don't have time to worry about suspects. Let's just concentrate on the Spider's Clue for now."

"You're right, Violet." Jessie tucked her long brown hair behind her ears. "Maybe if we put our heads together we can figure out what that line from the play means." She repeated it aloud to refresh everyone's memory. "*A rose by any other name would smell as sweet.*"

"If it's a line from a play," reasoned Benny, "that means the secret code word must have something to do with — "

"*Romeo and Juliet*," finished Violet.

"Or with Shakespeare," Jessie added.

But Henry wasn't so sure. "I think the key to the secret code word is in Sam's past," he said.

Jessie looked puzzled. "You really think so?" she asked.

"Well," replied Henry, "all the clues remind Sam of the past."

"So if the clues bring back memories for Sam," began Jessie, "that means maybe the millionaire — "

"Was someone Sam knew!" finished Benny.

Henry nodded. "I think so."

Jessie gave the matter some thought. If Henry was right, they would need to find out more about Sam's past.

Henry seemed to read her mind. "Maybe Sam will talk to us about the old days if we tell him how important it is."

"I wouldn't count on it, Henry," said Violet. She didn't think it was such a good idea to remind Sam of the past.

Then she thought of something.

"There *is* somebody we could ask."

"Who?" Benny was instantly curious.

"Thomas Paintner," replied Violet. "Remember what he told us?"

Henry nodded. "He said he's never too busy to see us."

Jessie looked at Henry. "Do you think he really meant it?"

"Well," said Henry, "there's only one way to find out."

CHAPTER 9

A Tangled Web

The Aldens pedaled downtown as fast as they could. They left their bikes in the parking lot behind the office building on Elm Street. As they raced around to the front of the building, they saw well-dressed people with briefcases coming and going.

The Aldens hurried inside the office building and up the stairs to the second floor. They walked along the hallway until they came to a door with PAINTNER AND BRADLEY written across the front in shiny black script.

As the door swung open, Melissa Campbell looked up from behind her desk.

"Hello, Melissa," Jessie said politely as they stepped inside. "Remember us?"

The woman's dark eyes narrowed in a frown. "Oh, yes." Her tone made it clear she wasn't pleased to see them.

"We came to visit Thomas," Benny piped up. Then he quickly added, "He told us it was okay."

"Mr. Paintner is busy with a client at the moment," Melissa replied in an icy voice. "Maybe you children should come back another time." She turned away.

But the Aldens didn't give up.

"We don't mind waiting," said Henry.

Melissa faced them again. "I'm afraid Mr. Paintner already has someone waiting."

When the children looked around, they noticed a young man sitting in the reception area. He was wearing a blue baseball cap with the letters GN on the front.

"We don't mind waiting, too," Henry said, a little more firmly this time. "We have all day."

He went and sat down in the reception area. Jessie, Violet, and Benny did the same.

Melissa glared over at them. "This is a place of business," she snapped, "not a playground."

"That's true," said Jessie, who refused to be rude. "And we'll try not to bother you."

Benny looked at Violet. "Wow," he said, his voice scarcely above a whisper. "Melissa doesn't like us very much, does she?"

But Violet was only half listening. Out of the corner of her eye, she was watching the man in the baseball cap. She remembered seeing him earlier that morning at the Hollow Tree Restaurant. But the more she looked at him, the more certain she was she'd seen him somewhere else, too. Where was it?

Just then Thomas Paintner stepped out of his office. He looked surprised to see the Aldens sitting in the reception area.

Thomas walked over to them, smiling. "What's up, kids?"

Henry got to his feet. So did his brother and sisters.

"We were hoping you might have time to talk," began Henry. "It's about — "

Melissa stood up so quickly, her chair scraped against the floor. "There's a gentleman here to see you," she broke in. "And he's been waiting for quite some time."

The man in the baseball cap suddenly stepped forward. "Ray Munch," he said, holding out his hand to Thomas. "I'm here about the inheritance."

The children could hardly believe their ears. They held their breath.

"What . . . ?" For a long moment, Thomas looked at the young man.

"I got this in the mail." Ray Munch reached into his pocket and pulled out an engraved invitation. He handed it to Thomas. "It says I'll get an inheritance if I come up with the right code word."

"You got this in the mail?" Thomas stared down at the invitation. He looked confused.

Jessie and Henry exchanged glances. Why did Thomas find it so hard to believe?

"You bet I did," replied Ray. "And I've got the code word all figured out."

Benny couldn't stand the suspense. "What is it?"

"*Shakespeare*," Ray said. "The secret code word is *Shakespeare!*"

Thomas shook his head. "That's not the secret code word at all."

The four Aldens let out the breath they'd been holding.

Ray Munch looked over at Melissa in surprise. "But . . . I was so sure."

The children caught the look. Thomas had seen it, too.

"What do you know about this, Melissa?" Thomas demanded.

Melissa looked angry. "How would I know anything about it?" she sputtered. "Why, I've never even seen that . . . that man before today."

Violet suddenly gasped. Everyone turned to look at her.

"What is it, Violet?" asked Henry.

"*I've* seen him before." Violet turned

to Ray Munch. "The letters on your ball cap . . ." She paused for a moment. " 'GN' stands for Greenfield Nursery. Right?"

"So what?" Ray shrugged. "What's it to you where I work?"

Benny suddenly recognized the man who'd almost bumped right into him. Putting his hands on his hips, the youngest Alden looked accusingly at Ray and Melissa. Then, turning to Thomas, he said, "We heard them at the nursery the other day. They were talking about a big chance for something."

"Is this true?" Thomas asked Melissa.

"I told you it wouldn't work," Ray muttered. "Didn't I tell you?" Then, without another word, he stormed out of the office.

Melissa's face turned a deep shade of red. She opened her mouth to speak, then closed it again. Suddenly her shoulders slumped, and she sat down in her chair, looking defeated.

"I think you have some explaining to do, Melissa," Thomas said in a stern voice.

After a moment's silence, Melissa began

to speak. "Ray Munch is my cousin," she confessed. Then she looked at Thomas. "I happened to pick up the phone the other day when you were talking to Sam Snow. He wanted to know if the invitation he got was genuine. You told him all about your client and the inheritance. When I heard you say you didn't know who was on your client's mailing list, it started me thinking."

Melissa told them the rest of the story. When Sam read the invitation aloud over the phone, she wrote it down word for word. Then she had an invitation made up for her cousin. Their agreement was to split the inheritance. It seemed like the perfect plan. The only hitch was getting hold of the clues. By a stroke of luck, though, Melissa met the Aldens. That's when she saw her chance.

"You stole my notebook," guessed Jessie. "And Grandfather's street map."

Melissa didn't deny it. For the first time she looked directly at the Aldens. "When you kids mentioned your boxcar, I decided to check it out. I thought I might find some clues for tracking down the secret code word." She paused. "I was only there long enough to grab the notebook and the map. I got out pretty fast."

Benny put in, "Only you broke the heel of your shoe getting away."

Melissa looked at Benny and nodded. She didn't seem surprised by what the Aldens knew. "I realized what good detectives you were when I looked through that notebook. Everything was in there. All Ray had to do was check out the spider plant at the restaurant." She let out a long, weary sigh. "I can't believe he botched it up."

"And I can't believe you actually stole from the Aldens," said Thomas, disappointment in his voice.

"I've done a lot of things I'm not very proud of," replied Melissa. She sounded sad.

Thomas shook his head. "I won't be needing your services anymore, Miss Campbell," he said. "Please clear out your desk as soon as possible."

Just then the door opened. Sam Snow and Rose Hill stepped inside.

Sam was wearing his best shirt and pants, while Rose was dressed in pink again. Even her purse had a pink rose on the front.

As Benny looked over at the owner of the Hollow Tree Restaurant, he suddenly figured out the answer to one mystery. His mouth dropped open.

Rose Hill was Pinky!

CHAPTER 10

The Mystery Man

"We thought we'd take you out for lunch with us, Thomas," said Rose. "And what a stroke of luck to find the Aldens here!" she added, glancing over at the children.

"We'd sure like it if you'd join us," Sam told them.

The children looked at one another. They would never be able to discuss Sam's past with Sam right there.

Thomas spoke up before they could answer. "I just have a few things to clear off my desk." He opened his door a crack. "Why don't we step inside my office for a minute." He was almost shouting. "It'll be more comfortable."

Thomas was usually so soft-spoken. Violet wondered why he was raising his voice.

"No need to yell, Thomas," said Rose, who seemed to think it odd, too. "We're right here."

They stepped inside a cozy office where law books filled the shelves and chairs were clustered before a huge desk. On the far side of the room was a door leading to an adjoining office.

Violet moved closer to her younger brother. "What's the matter, Benny?" She knew by the look on his face that something was up.

"I know who Pinky is!" Benny announced. And he glanced meaningfully over at Rose.

Henry, Jessie, and Violet exchanged looks of amazement.

"Rose Hill is Pinky?" whispered Violet in disbelief.

"How did you know?" Rose couldn't help laughing when she overheard. "Pinky was my nickname when I was a young girl." Then she added, "But nobody's called me that in years."

Thomas laughed along with Rose as he sat down at his desk. "Back then, that's all we ever called you!"

"Didn't know you had any other name in the old days," added Sam.

Henry looked at Jessie. Jessie nodded back. She was thinking what he was thinking. Rose was an old friend of Sam's. They'd known each other for years. It all added up. The key to the code word really *was* in Sam's past — and the key was Rose Hill!

"*A rose by any other name would smell as sweet!*" said Jessie.

Violet gasped. "And a rose by any other name is 'Pinky'!"

"That must be the secret code word," concluded Henry. "Is that it?" he asked Thomas. "Is the secret code word — 'Pinky'?"

Thomas reached into a drawer and removed an envelope. Opening the flap, he pulled out a small card. Then he held it up for everyone to see. The word PINKY appeared on it in large type.

A slow smile spread across the lawyer's face. "You hit the nail on the head, kids!"

"Didn't I tell you they were fine detectives?" said Sam, his eyes shining.

Just then Violet heard something — a slight shuffling sound. It seemed to be coming from behind the door of the adjoining office. Was someone listening through the door? Melissa had told them Thomas was busy with a client. But where was his client? Violet had no time to think about it, though. Thomas was talking again.

"You children did a fine job," he said. "And just in the nick of time, too."

Henry nodded, but he looked troubled. Something just didn't feel right.

"What is it, Henry?" asked Jessie.

Everyone turned to look at him.

"I'm not sure," said Henry. "But it's like Grandfather said — it's such an amazing coincidence."

"Coincidence?" Sam raised an eyebrow as he sat down in a chair.

"Don't you think it's strange," said Henry, "that this inheritance came along just when you're out of work, Sam?"

"Well," Sam said thoughtfully, "now that you mention it . . ."

"And the lawyer handling the estate just happens to be a friend of yours," added Henry. "That's a pretty big coincidence, too. Don't you think?"

Sam nodded. So did Violet and Benny.

Jessie nodded, too. But she was thinking of something else. "And then there's the code word itself," she said. "Only a few people would have known Rose's nickname."

"Hmm, I hadn't thought of that," Sam said.

"Why were you so surprised, Thomas," Henry asked, "when Ray Munch said he was here about the inheritance?"

The question seemed to catch Thomas off guard. "What . . . ?"

Henry quickly explained to Sam and Rose

what had happened before their arrival. Then he turned to Thomas again. "You seemed so sure Ray Munch was up to something. It was almost as if you knew, somehow, that his name wasn't on the millionaire's mailing list."

Thomas shifted uncomfortably in his chair. "I had a hunch, that's all."

"There's another strange coincidence," said Violet. "The person who came up with these clues must have liked mysteries. And he was good at making them up, too. Just like you, Thomas."

Benny folded his arms. "That's right." He looked accusingly at Thomas. "You make up codes and clues for your grandchildren. I bet you made up this mystery, too!"

Thomas held up a hand. "Wait a minute!"

Sam looked sharply at his old friend. "What's going on, Thomas?"

There was a long silence. In a quiet voice, Thomas finally answered Sam's question. "I guess you've found me out," he said. "The mystery of the Spider's Clue was my own invention."

Sam blinked in disbelief. "You tricked me?"

"I did."

"Oh, dear." Rose wrung her hands. "Things aren't going the way we'd planned."

Sam turned to her in surprise. "You were in on this, too?" He sounded more hurt than angry.

"Well . . ." Rose began, then stopped. She managed a weak smile. "We were just trying to help."

At that moment, the door of the adjoining office swung open. A heavyset man with silver hair stood in the doorway.

Jessie gasped. "The mystery man!"

Sam's mouth had dropped open. "It . . . it can't be!"

"You were listening at the door," Violet said suspiciously. "Who are you?"

Thomas smiled at the Aldens. "Well, kids," he said, "I'd like to introduce you to Sam's brother, Simon Snow."

"What?" the Aldens all cried at once.

"Yes, it's true," Simon admitted. "I was here visiting Thomas. When I heard everyone coming inside, I hid in the other room."

Violet nodded. That explained why Thomas had raised his voice after opening the door a crack. He was warning Simon to duck out of sight.

Simon looked over at his brother. "Don't be angry with Rose. Or with Thomas. This whole thing was my idea."

"It was your idea to trick me?" Sam looked upset.

Rose put a hand on Sam's arm. "Simon only wanted to help. He heard about your accident, Sam. He knew you'd be too proud to accept money from him. Between the three of us, we came up with this elaborate scheme to help you out."

Sam was confused. "Then there never was an inheritance?"

"That's right," answered Simon.

"Or a butler who sent out invitations," added Henry.

"Right again," said Simon. "Sam was the only one who received an invitation in the mail."

"And I sent that out myself," put in Thomas. "The money wasn't an inheritance. It was a gift from Simon." Then he looked over at the Aldens and shook his head. "I knew you children were good detectives. But I had no idea you'd figure out so much."

Jessie had some questions. The mystery was still not fully explained. "We overheard you on the phone, Simon," she said, "when we were tracking down clues. You mentioned the mystery, and you sounded upset."

Simon and Rose looked at each other.

"Oh, that must've been when Simon phoned me," said Rose. "We were arguing about the mystery. I was certain you'd never find the Hollow Tree Restaurant. I mean, the sign's so faded on the awning. I thought we should give you a hint or two. But Simon wouldn't hear of it. He was certain we'd be sorry if we said anything. He thought it would just make you suspicious."

"I knew you could solve it on your own," said Simon. "I saw you in the library one day, browsing through nursery rhymes. I knew you were going to solve the mystery just fine."

"Were you following us?" asked Benny.

Simon shook his head. "I'm sorry if I frightened you. I was passing by and I saw you go inside. I was just curious to see if your visit to the library had anything to do with the mystery."

"If the Aldens hadn't seen through your plan, Simon, you would have left Greenfield without speaking to me." Sam's expression was grim. "Isn't that true?"

Simon hung his head. "I stood outside your house one afternoon, Sam," he confessed. "I tried to work up the courage to knock on your door."

"I saw you there," Jessie said quietly.

Simon nodded. "I wanted to see you again, Sam. But I was afraid you'd turn me away."

"Turn you away?" Sam looked shocked.

"I would never turn my own brother away!"

Simon Snow crossed the room. He put out his hand. Sam got slowly to his feet, and the two men shook hands, then embraced.

Simon had tears in his eyes. "I've been such a fool."

"That makes two of us, Simon," Sam said in a choked voice. "That makes two of us."

Sam was true to his word. Just as soon as he was back on his feet, he cooked a big pot of chili and invited everyone over to enjoy it with him — the four Alden children, Grandfather Alden, Mrs. McGregor, Simon, Thomas, and Rose. And, of course, Watch.

"I still can't believe it," said Sam, shaking his head. "I never thought I'd see the day my brother would be sitting right here in my kitchen." Sam looked happier than the Aldens had ever seen him.

"Well, you'd better get used to it," said Simon as he helped himself to another bowl of chili. "I'll be retiring next month, and I can't think of a better place to spend my

retirement years than right here in Greenfield."

Grandfather Alden smiled. "It's a wonderful town."

Simon sat back in his chair. "Years ago, I told my brother he was making a big mistake to come back to Greenfield. But I was wrong." He turned to Sam. "You live in a town where everyone loves and respects you. I envy you for that. I just wish . . ." Simon paused. "I just wish you'd let me help you out, Sam. I've done really well in the carpet business, you know."

Sam suddenly got up from the table. He walked across the room and opened a drawer. When he came back to the table, he was holding his bank book. "Take a look at my savings account, Simon," he said.

Simon let out a low whistle when he saw the balance. "I had no idea you were doing so well, Sam."

Sam nodded. "I've worked hard all these years. And I haven't had many needs."

Rose clapped her hands. "The Three Musketeers have all done well for themselves," she said. "And I'll expect to see all three of you at the Hollow Tree! Especially now that it's getting spruced up a bit," she added.

"Did the bank approve your loan?" asked Thomas.

Rose nodded happily. Then she looked over at the Aldens. "That's the reason I was tottering around in those high heels the day I met you. I had an appointment with the bank manager and I was trying to make a good impression — I guess it worked."

Violet smiled. She knew Rose could never have stolen from anybody.

"Thanks to the Aldens, everything's turned out great for all of us!" Sam said.

"And thanks to Watch," added Violet. "He helped solve the mystery."

"He sure did," agreed Henry.

Watch barked when he heard his name. "Woof, woof!"

"Don't worry." Benny gave their little dog a hug. "Another mystery will come along soon. You can count on it!"

GERTRUDE CHANDLER WARNER discovered when she was teaching that many readers who like an exciting story could find no books that were both easy and fun to read. She decided to try to meet this need, and her first book, *The Boxcar Children*, quickly proved she had succeeded.

Miss Warner drew on her own experiences to write the mystery. As a child she spent hours watching trains go by on the tracks opposite her family home. She often dreamed about what it would be like to set up housekeeping in a caboose or freight car — the situation the Alden children find themselves in.

When Miss Warner received requests for more adventures involving Henry, Jessie, Violet, and Benny Alden, she began additional stories. In each, she chose a special setting and introduced unusual or eccentric characters who liked the unpredictable.

While the mystery element is central to each of Miss Warner's books, she never thought of them as strictly juvenile mysteries. She liked to stress the Aldens' independence and resourcefulness and their solid New England devotion to using up and making do. The Aldens go about most of their adventures with as little adult supervision as possible — something else that delights young readers.

Miss Warner lived in Putnam, Connecticut, until her death in 1979. During her lifetime, she received hundreds of letters from girls and boys telling her how much they liked her books.